NUDE CRUISE

AN EROTIC ADVENTURE

VICTORIA RUSH

VOLUME 4

JADE'S EROTIC ADVENTURES - BOOK 4

COPYRIGHT

Nude Cruise © 2018 Victoria Rush

Cover Design © 2018 PhotoMaras

All Rights Reserved

Some people can get into pretty tight spots on a crowded train...

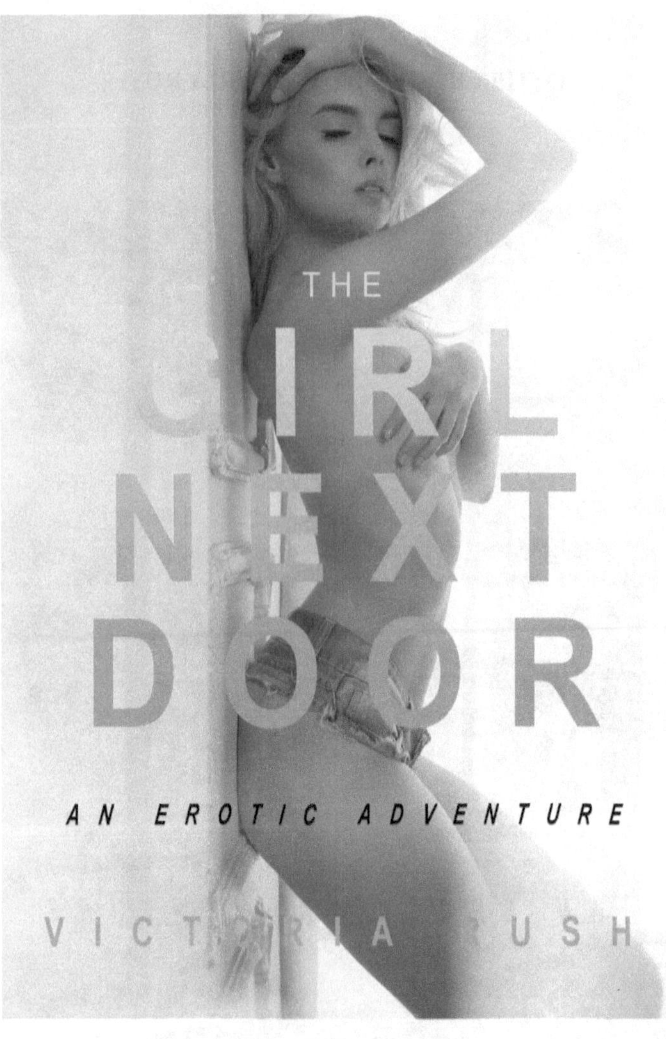

Everyone's an exhibitionist in disguise...

GIRLS' CAMP

AN EROTIC ADVENTURE

VICTORIA RUSH

Getting wet was never this much fun...

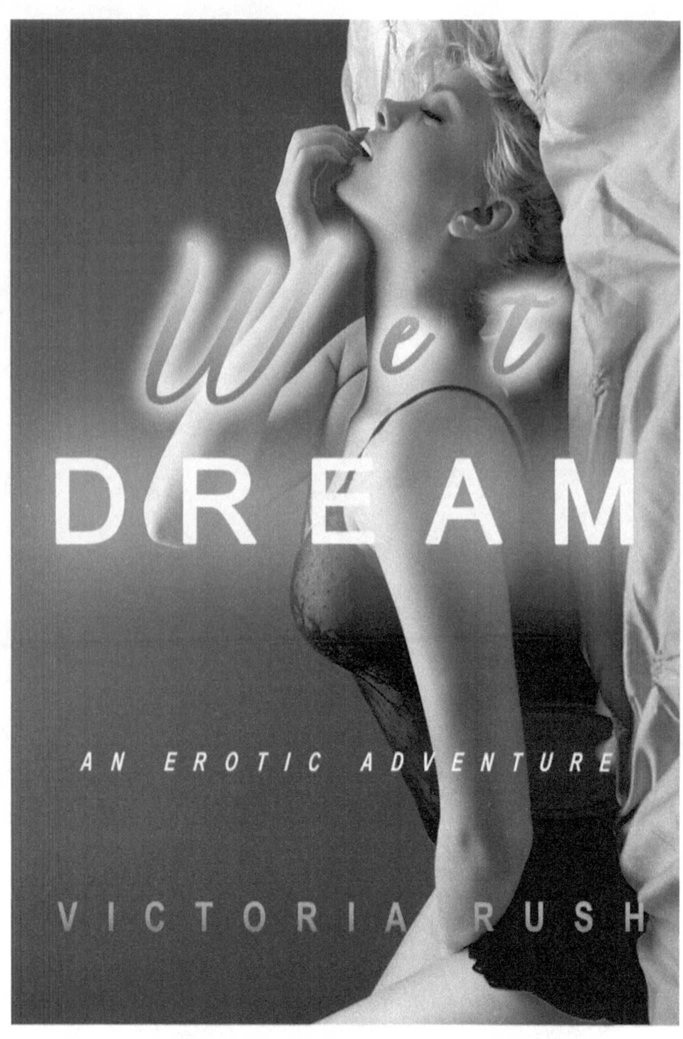

There's only one place you can live out your wildest fantasies...

Jade's EROTIC ADVENTURES

BOOKS 1 - 5

VICTORIA RUTH

The complete five-book bestselling series — 60% off

For the uninhibited...

1

—————

EXOTIC VOYAGE

My exhilarating encounters at the dinner party, the dark room, and naked yoga had whet my appetite for new adventures. But each of these experiences, as stimulating and fulfilling as they were in their own right, were one-time affairs. In each case, it hadn't taken long for me to yearn for something new, something more. I wanted an *all-in-one* adventure, where I could move from one new experience to another without having to search for the next one. I wanted my own erotic *Disneyland*.

I knew if I could find such diverse activities online, there must be a whole underworld of swingers looking for something similar. Surely some enterprising operator would see the potential in putting together some kind of package deal. I sat down in front of my computer, opened up my browser, and typed in the words 'all-inclusive erotic adventure.'

A surprising number of 'clothing-optional' resort listings came up. I clicked on the first one, but it just showed the usual pictures of pretty pools, beaches, and guests suites, with a vague description of an 'upscale retreat for an adventurous lifestyle experience'. A little further down the page, I saw a blog article titled *Inside a nudist sex resort*. The article described an adventure traveler's experience at a resort where couples romped on nude beaches, swam in nude pools, and 'hooked up' in private cabins.

Definitely a little too tame-sounding for me.

I clicked on the next page of search results, where I saw a link titled *Nude Cruise — Explore Your Erotic Fantasies*.

This looks interesting.

I clicked on the link and a webpage opened showing pictures of naked people climbing walls, dancing in water fountains, and wrestling in a muddy pit.

That looks a little different, I thought.

At the top of the webpage, there was a tab titled *Fantasy Menu*. I clicked on the link, and a list of sexy-sounding shipboard activities appeared:

> Peak Sensation
> House of Holes
> Fantasy Fountain
> Sensuous Steam Room
> Masquerade Ball
> Sexy Games Room
> Get Down Disco
> Cybersex Rules
> Private View Rooms
> Intimate Massage
> FourPlay

I clicked on the first one and a photo appeared showing naked men and women scaling a climbing wall with unusual foot and hand holds. Instead of the usual jug and pocket holds, the 'grips' were in the shape of dildos and artificial vaginas, where climbers could pause to 'rest' and 'recharge their batteries' as they scaled the wall. A description under the photo read:

Challenge yourself to a climbing wall like no other. The higher you go, the more stimulating the experience becomes. Reward yourself at each new level, where you'll find a new wall feature to stimulate and excite every part of your body, as you seek the peak experience at the top of the mountain. All while safely strapped into a comfortable harness that permits a maximum range of movement and accessibility.

That sounds like an incredible turn on, I thought.

The idea of fucking a dildo strapped to a wall while people watched me from below sounded insanely sexy. My pussy began to twitch as I imagined the idea.

What's this next one—*House of Holes*?

I clicked on the next listed activity, and a picture appeared showing various nude men and women pressing their hips and buttocks against a wall with scattered holes. The look of ecstasy on their faces left little doubt as to what was happening on the other side. The description read:

Hook up with a stranger on the other side of a wall through your own personal intimate portal. You can choose to 'give', 'receive', or 'merge' with a partner of either sex in an erotic and completely anonymous connection. Or you can choose to simply watch, as other couples get their groove on in this sensuous and erotic House of Holes.

Damn, that sounds dirty. And fun.

I'd heard of glory holes before, but I'd always thought of them as skanky places where gay men went to get an anony-mous blow job. The idea of engaging in heterosexual sex or touching pussies with another woman through my own private portal was different. And highly stimulating. My left hand dropped down between my legs and I began to rub my clit as I continued exploring the website.

What happens in the Sexy Games Room?

I clicked on the next activity, which displayed a photo of naked men and women in contorted positions atop a polka-dot-covered mat. Their hips and asses were pressed together while they stretched their arms and legs around each other. The caption read:

Play interactive nude games with your fellow guests where the rules and rewards are wide open. With Naked Twister, stretch into increasingly difficult and erotic positions as you try to reach around, over, and under your naked partners. Or try Naked Poker where the 'loser' must engage in increasingly erotic situations in full view of their playing partners. Or jump into the Naked Mud Wrestling pit and try to wrestle your partner into submission, all while surrounded in sensuous mud.

Fuck, yes! I thought. *These guys know how to organize an erotic party.*

I didn't need to click any more of the fantasy activities to know this was the sort of erotic travel destination that I had in mind. It promised to be an immersive, stimulating experience with multiple partners and exciting activities. As always though, I needed to be sure it would be clean and safe. I searched the page and found a tab marked *Conditions*, which read:

Every Nude Cruise guest must provide a certified report from a verified medical testing lab, indicating negative for sexually communicated diseases. The report must be dated within one week of your ship's departure date. Clothing is optional for all activities. Security staff are available at all venues to ensure the safety of guests and to ensure that all interaction occurs only with express consent.

Fair enough, I thought. *The medical test requirement shows this is a class act. You can't be too careful about these things.*

I clicked the Booking tab and viewed the calendar for available dates. The next cruise departed from Miami in two weeks' time. I'd have to move a few things around and schedule a two-hour flight, but one of the joys of my job as a freelance graphic designer meant I could choose my own vacation days. I booked a private cabin with a Queen-size bed, then I tore my panties off and plunged my fingers into my pussy as I fantasized about all the shipboard activities I'd soon be participating in.

2

———

SETTING SAIL

On the scheduled day of my departure, my whole body was buzzing with excitement. This was my first cruise, and I didn't know what to expect. Besides my fear of seasickness, I was a little nervous about the idea of parading around nude in public. I'd picked up some anti-nausea pills at the pharmacy, but I had butterflies in my stomach for an entirely different reason.

So far, my excursions into the realm of public sex and nudity had been fairly anonymous. At the dinner party, I could hide behind my masquerade mask. In the dark room, the special light effects concealed my identity. Even at my naked yoga class, everybody was so busy concentrating on their poses that it was really only my partner who had a close-up view of me.

But on this 'clothing-optional' cruise, I'd be going about my everyday routines in plain view of hundreds of strangers. Granted, some of the activities sounded highly erotic and fun. But the idea of sitting down for dinner or even just sunbathing in the nude gave me the willies. I'd packed some skimpy bikinis in case I got cold feet, but I didn't want to be the only one wearing clothes if everyone else was naked.

When I arrived at the cruise terminal, it was a hive of activity. There were hundreds of people waiting to go through security, and the building was buzzing with chatter and public announcements. I pulled out my boarding pass and looked for the sign directing me to my designated gate. Just like at airport security, there were multiple lines of people placing their bags on conveyor belts going through an X-ray machine. When it was my turn, I took off my shoes and opened my roller-bag to remove my liquids.

"That won't be necessary, ma'am," a handsome security attendant said.

"Oh?" I murmured, confused.

"No need to remove your shoes or any items from your bag," he said. "Security procedures for cruise ships aren't as stringent as they are for air travel."

I smiled and nodded sheepishly as I pulled my sandals back on.

"Unless you're carrying something metal, of course. That'll set our machine off."

"No, of course not," I said, blushing from all the attention I was getting holding up the line. But now I was worried about the vibrator I'd packed in my luggage.

Who needs to bring a vibrator on a naked sex cruise, anyway? I chided myself.

"I'll just need to see your boarding pass," the security agent said.

I showed him my pass, and he directed me to stand in line behind the pass-through body scanner. As I waited for my turn, I looked around at my fellow boarding passengers. Most of them were fairly young, in their 20s and 30s, but there were also some older couples who were apparently looking for a little adventure to spice up their marriages. I noticed a few people checking each other out. Most of them didn't make eye contact for very long, but I wasn't the only one undressing some of the hot passengers with my eyes.

I caught a tanned gentleman in the adjacent line running his eyes up and down my body. I'd intentionally worn skinny jeans and a tight blouse for the first day to show off my best assets. I stood up tall and lifted my chest to display my cleavage. He had a nice ass, strong arms, and beautiful skin. When our eyes met, he smiled at me, and I could feel the blood rushing to my face again.

Come on, Jade, I admonished myself. *Get a hold of yourself. If you're going to be this self-conscious fully clothed, how are you ever going to be comfortable walking around in the nude?*

I returned my attention to the X-ray machine as my bag disappeared under the cover. I watched the face of the security agent as he scanned the monitor for any suspicious contents, then breathed a sigh of relief when I saw my bag pop out the other end.

"Ma'am?" the agent at the opposite side of the body scanner said, motioning for me to step through.

I'd been so worried my vibrator would set off the X-ray machine, that I hadn't realized I was holding up the line again. I nodded self-consciously, then walked through the pass-through stand, making eye contact with the security agent to ensure I wouldn't set off any other alarms. After he nodded that I was clear, I picked my bag off the X-ray belt and looked for the sign to the check-in area. By now, I was sure that half the passengers in the security area were cursing in bewilderment at my awkward travel etiquette, and I was glad to find a respite at the end of a new line.

"That's a pretty big bag for a short cruise," a woman's voice said, as I heard someone step up behind me.

I turned around and looked into the eyes of a stunning brunette about my same height.

"Um, well, you know," I stammered. "It's mostly makeup and toiletries and that sort of thing. We women can't be shorthanded about these things."

I could feel the flush in my cheeks again, caught off guard by her disarming beauty.

"No, I suppose not," she said, smiling at my innocence. "Although something tells me *makeup* will be the least of our concerns on this trip."

Her confidence and bold manner was rapidly sending blood flowing to another part of my body.

"Is this your first time with this cruise operator?" I asked, not wanting to state the obvious.

"This is my third Fantasy Cruise. Once you dip your toes in, it's kind of addicting." Her eyes darted across my face, appraising my demeanor. "How about you?"

"It's my first time. I'm a bit nervous, to be honest. You know, about all the..."

"Yeah, there's a lot of that," she said. "But there's nothing to worry about. We're all in the same boat, so to speak. You get used to it pretty fast. It's actually quite liberating. Not having to dress up and put on airs. Nudity is a great equalizer."

I took a quick glance at her tight and tanned body. She was wearing loose fitting linen shorts and a tight T-shirt displaying a cruise ship sailing into the sunset. Her legs were long and shapely, and her firm breasts sat up high on her chest.

"Some of us are a little more equal than others, I'm afraid."

She scanned my figure and smiled.

"I don't think you have anything to worry about. You're

gorgeous. As long as you don't mind being the center of attention with a body like that."

I puffed out my cheeks and exhaled heavily.

"That's exactly what I'm worried about. I'm not used to being the center of attention. At least not in a public setting with all my clothes off."

"What deck is your cabin on?" she asked.

I fumbled for my travel papers and pulled out my boarding pass.

"E deck," I said. "They told me that if I chose a cabin nearer the water line, I have a better chance of avoiding seasickness."

"That's my deck too. Stick with me girl, and I'll show you around. There are plenty of ways to take your mind off the motion of the boat. The key is to not stay in one place too long. With so many interesting shipboard activities, your stomach will be the *last* thing you'll be thinking about."

She held out her hand and smiled at me.

"My name's Heather."

"Jade," I said, shaking her hand softly. "Thanks, Heather. I could use a wing woman, or shipmate, or whatever you're supposed to call your cruise partner these days."

"It's a deal," Heather said, winking at me. "We'll be *partners in crime*."

I reached the front of the line and saw one of the check-in agents motioning for me to come to her station.

"I'll wait for you past check-in," I said, suddenly mindful of the increasing dampness building between my legs.

3

———

RECEPTION

After clearing through Check-in, Heather guided me through the final boarding process then we walked together toward our rooms on E deck. We agreed to meet thirty minutes later when we'd go to the guest reception in the main lounge on the top deck. Our rooms were in the same hall, so after saying temporary goodbyes, I continued down the hall toward my stateroom.

When I opened my door, I was surprised by how small my room was. The Queen-size bed seemed to take up almost all of the space, with a tiny adjoining closet and small desk beside the wall-mounted TV. I went into the bathroom and was disappointed to see a stand-up shower with no tub. I knew that space aboard a cruise ship was at a premium, but I wasn't expecting it to feel so claustrophobic.

I unpacked my toiletries and placed them on the tiny sink, then carried my small carry-on case and placed it on the bed. There was a small sliding window beside my bed, and I immediately walked over and slid it open to breathe in some fresh air. I could see a flotilla of small boats moving about the bay opposite our ship, and I immediately regretted not upgrading to a larger room with balcony.

I bet Heather has a bigger room, I thought. *I'm such a lightweight at this cruise thing.*

I was looking forward to picking her brain for other tips about optimizing my shipboard experience. Not to mention picking over the *rest* of her body. I couldn't wait to see her naked and run my hands over her tight ass and breasts.

The porter had taken my larger roller case, and I didn't have much of a change of clothes in my carry-on bag. Heather had said not to worry too much about what to wear for the reception since most first-time guests chose not to go fully nude at the first activity. Nevertheless, I wanted to get with the program and ease myself into the idea of being naked on board, so I removed my bra and unbuttoned my silk blouse three buttons to reveal my cleavage.

I went into the washroom and looked at myself in the small mirror. The soft silk rubbing against my nipples had already stimulated them to an aroused state, and they protruded against the thin fabric, creating two conspicuous nodes. I smiled at how full and firm my breasts looked in my revealing blouse and hoped they'd attract Heather's attention too. I put on a new coat of light red lipstick and touched up my mascara, then grabbed my purse and headed down the hall toward Heather's room.

When she opened her door and I saw what she was wearing, it took my breath away. She wore a see-through gauzy top that barely concealed her large breasts through the sheer material. I stared shamelessly at her figure, wanting to flip her loose top up over her waist and devour her firm, round tits. To top it off, she'd let her long brown hair down and it shone with iridescent hues of amber and gold. She looked absolutely ravishing, and I was already regretting my wardrobe choice.

"Damn, girl," I said. "You're a feast for sore eyes. Who needs hors d'oeuvres when the main course is standing right here in front of me."

"That can be arranged," she said. "Come on in. Let's freshen up before heading over to the reception."

Heather motioned me into her room and I stepped inside. As I suspected, her room was larger than mine, with a small sitting room next to her bed and French doors leading out to a balcony.

"I knew I should have upgraded to a suite," I frowned. "I'm already beginning to feel claustrophobic in my tiny little cabin."

I looked out her French doors toward the open bay.

"Do you mind if I check out your view?"

"Of course. Make yourself comfortable. You're welcome to hang at my place anytime you're feeling closed in. I'll just be a couple more minutes."

Heather disappeared into the washroom, and I slid the side doors open and stepped out onto her balcony. I could smell the fresh salty air from the sea and I closed my eyes as I breathed it in.

This is definitely the way to travel, I thought. *Next time,* I reminded myself, *remember to get a full-size suite with balcony.*

After a few minutes, Heather emerged from the washroom looking even more beautiful than before, and I couldn't help shaking my head.

"I'm feeling terribly overdressed. You look like you're getting in the swing of this nude cruise thing already. Should I find something skimpier to wear?"

"Nonsense," Heather said. "You look perfect." Her eyes traced a line down to my aroused nipples protruding against my blouse. "You're revealing just the right amount for the meet and greet. I guarantee you'll be getting a lot of attention in that tight outfit."

I glanced down at her tanned legs and sandals.

"But you're showing a lot more...skin. Am I going to be the only one covering up my whole body?"

"Not at all. Most first-timers come to the initial reception dressed pretty conservative. It takes a couple of days for people to get comfortable being in the buff around their fellow passengers. By the second or third day, everybody will be strolling around buck naked. After the reception there's a dance, where the lights get turned down. You'll have plenty of opportunity to shed some of your clothes then."

As Heather walked toward me, I watched her breasts jiggle under her sheer blouse. When she stood in front of me, I stared at her tits and soft brown nipples. I couldn't stop myself.

"May I?" I said, looking gently into her eyes.

"I thought you'd never ask," she smiled.

I lifted her top and cupped her breasts in my hands and squeezed them softly. They were full and firm, and perfectly shaped, straight out of a centerfold. I noticed her areolas contract and her nipples begin to extend. I rolled them gently between my thumbs and forefingers, and she leaned in to kiss me. When our lips met, I pushed my body toward hers and pressed my hips against hers. She grabbed the back of my head and pulled me closer as our tongues danced around each other's mouths. I could have fucked her right then and there, but after a long lingering kiss, she pulled away.

"There'll be plenty of time for this later," she said. "Let's go meet some new people at the reception. This is a *nude cruise*, remember? We don't want to be holed up in our cabin the whole time, do we?"

"I suppose not," I said, slightly disappointed. My head knew she was right, but the ache in my pussy disagreed. I wanted her right now, and I didn't feel like sharing her with anybody else.

"Come on," she said, grabbing my hand, pulling me toward the door. "Let's go trip the night fantastic."

When we got to the top deck, Heather led me to a large open lounge with floor-to-ceiling windows offering a commanding view of the bay. I hadn't realized the ship had already left the pier, and I saw that we were steaming past South Pointe Park toward the open sea.

There were hundreds of people milling around the room, and Heather clasped my hand as she led me toward the bar. I was glad almost everybody was fully clothed, ranging from shorts and T-shirts to camisoles and bikini bottoms. A few veteran Fantasy Cruise travelers had been bold enough to go topless, but for the most part, it was a fairly low-key affair.

"What'll you have, ladies?" a handsome bartender wearing a white dress shirt and bowtie asked.

"I'll have a watermelon vodka," I said.

"I'd like some sex on the beach please," Heather said.

"Coming right up," the bartender smiled.

"You're so naughty," I teased Heather.

"Hey, when in Rome..." she said.

I turned and looked around the room. Heather had given me good advice about what to wear, and I began to feel more relaxed.

"You were right about the dress code tonight," I said. "Though the bartender seems a little formal. Are the staff always dressed so prim and proper?"

"They're always *dressed*, if that's what you mean. It's company policy that staff always must wear clothes, even on a nude cruise. Something about maintaining their professionalism, I suppose. It kind of helps to separate the staff from the guests, especially when you need something. The officers dress in navy whites, and the servers typically wear black pants, vests, and bow ties."

I watched the bartender approach us as he returned from the other end of the bar.

"Are they allowed to...you know...*hook up* with guests?" I asked.

"Officially it's a no-no, but whatever enterprising staff chooses to do when they're off duty, is nobody's business. If they get caught cavorting with passengers they can technically be fired, but it's pretty hard not to dip your toe in the water every now and then with so many flirty naked passengers floating around."

"I see your point," I said, as a pretty topless girl walked past us.

"Here you go, ladies," the bartender said, placing our drinks in front of us.

"Come on," Heather said, picking up her glass. "Let's go mingle."

For the next hour or so, Heather and I stuck together as we wandered from one cluster of passengers to another, making small talk. Nobody seemed to want to address the elephant in the room, mostly sticking with safe subjects like where we were from, what we did for a living, and if we'd been on a Fantasy Cruise before.

But everybody was definitely checking each other out.

Although most of us were technically fully 'dressed', there was plenty enough skin showing to get a good idea of what we'd look like naked. Most of the men wore tight T-shirts or open shirts, revealing plenty of chiseled pecs and abs. The women wore skimpy bikinis, or flimsy camisoles and miniskirts. It was a feast for the eyes, and I soaked it all in. After a little while, I spotted the tall gentleman who I'd made eye contact with in the security line, and I gently steered Heather in his direction.

"I see you managed to survive the security gauntlet," he said to me, as I shimmied up next to him.

"Barely," I laughed. "I wasn't sure who was going to arrest me first—the security guards for my smuggled contraband or the passengers who were steaming about me holding up the line."

"It wasn't so bad," he smiled. "Traveling on a ship is easier than a plane. Is this your first time?"

"Yes," I said. "How about you?"

"This is my second trip. I guess I had some unfinished business from my first time around. There's so much to do on this big ship—one week hardly seems to be enough time to take it all in."

I paused for a moment as I appraised his body. He was wearing creme-colored linen pants and sandals, with a loose-fitting short-sleeved Bermuda shirt. But it was unbuttoned enough to show the cleft rippling between his chiseled pecs as he motioned with his powerful arms. His dark eyes beckoned to me, as I began to fantasize about falling into his arms.

"I'm Marc," he said, extending his hand.

"Jade," I said, feeling his large fingers envelop me. I turned toward Heather. "And this is my partner in crime, Heather."

Marc smiled as he looked at Heather, trying to keep his gaze concentrated above her barely concealed breasts.

"Are you two sisters?" he said. "Because I have seen such a lovely pair since Giselle and Patricia Bundchen."

"If you're talking about Jade and me," Heather teased, "no." Then she grabbed her breasts and shook them provocatively. "But if you're talking about my girls here, I'll take that as a compliment."

"Either way," Marc said, "I mean it as a compliment."

A woman's voice suddenly came over the room's public address system to break the sexual tension. The three of us turned toward the stage, where a woman wearing white shorts and a pressed shirt was standing holding a mic.

"Good evening, Fantasy Cruise travelers!" she said, raising her voice in welcome.

A loud cheer filled the room from the attending guests.

"My name's Ashley, and I'll be your cruise director. For those of you who are traveling on your maiden voyage with Fantasy Cruise, welcome. And for those of you returning for more fun and games, I promise you won't be disappointed. We've added even more fantasy activities to uplift and stimulate you.

"All of you should have found the brochure with our full Fantasy Menu on your nightstand when you checked into your staterooms, but we have lots more here on the desk beside the stage. Whenever you have any questions, just come see me any time. I'll be here the rest of the evening, and you can find my office mid-ship next to the Poseidon Restaurant on Deck B. Or just ring me at triple-two on your in-room phone.

"But now, let's get this party started with our first Fantasy Dance!" she hollered.

The suddenly lights dimmed and flashing lights began

circulating the room. The sound of Marvin Gaye's *Let's Get it On* began booming over the speakers, and Heather, Marc and I began swaying our hips together in unison. Heather turned toward me and began shaking her ass suggestively in Marc's direction.

He's dreamy! she mouthed to me.

Damn straight, I returned, widening my eyes in agreement.

Marc simply smiled at me as he pretended to grind his hips against Heather's ass.

My first fantasy cruise was off to a promising start.

4

GETTING DOWN

For the next hour or so, Heather, Marc and I got our groove on as the swirling lights from the disco ball flashed over the writhing crowd. With the sun beginning to set over the horizon, the room became increasingly dark, and some brave passengers began shedding their clothes. Heather was the first to take off her skimpy top, and after another ten minutes of bumping and grinding with her and Marc, I soon followed suit. Not long after, Marc ripped off his shirt and threw it on a growing pile beside the stage.

It felt fabulous to be semi-nude, and we shamelessly rubbed our bodies together as the sexy music played in the background. It didn't take long for us to remove our clothes completely as we got more and more worked up by the suggestive lyrics. When Donna Summer's *Love to Love You Baby* came over the speakers, we moved in close and rolled our hips and chests together, our passion rising in tandem with the singer's orgiastic moans. I could feel Marc's cock hardening against our bodies as my wetness commingled with Heather's on our skin. As usual, Heather made the first move.

"Let's get out of here," she panted in our ears, and we didn't even bother to pick up our clothes as the three of us pranced out of the lounge. Bypassing the elevator, Heather led the way down the closest stairwell while we raced down the three flights to E deck. We giggled our way down the hall past a few other half-dressed passengers as we headed toward Heather's room. When we got to her door, I looked at her blankly, wondering how we were going to get in. We were all stark naked, and none of us were carrying a room key.

"Shit!" I said to Heather. "What now? Maybe we can find a secluded spot on the deck—"

"Not to worry," she said. "I've been in this predicament before, and I've taken precautions."

She kneeled down on the floor and peered through the small crack under the base of her door. Then she reached into the space with her fingers and pulled a credit-card-sized room key out across the carpet.

"Shazam!" she said, standing up and displaying her room key triumphantly. "A lady is prepared for every contingency."

She fumbled with the key in the lock then pushed open the door, and the three of us scrambled into her room. As soon as the door closed, Heather jumped up onto Marc and threw her legs around his hips. He turned and pinned her against the door, and they started kissing passionately. I rubbed my breasts against his sweaty back and moved my hand between his legs. I could feel his hard cock pointing down between Heather's legs, and I rubbed it against her soaking pussy. It didn't take long for the three of us to be coated in her slippery juices.

I squeezed Marc's balls gently as he contracted his glutes

and pressed harder against Heather. All three of us were panting, wanting a piece of his meat. Suddenly, he swung around and carried Heather toward the bed with her still clinging to his hips. He placed one knee on the bed and lowered her onto its surface, then pressed his body against hers. Not wanting to interrupt their rhythm, I stood and watched as my sticky hand moved between my legs.

At this point, I was so turned on I could have come just watching Heather and Marc make love. But Heather had other plans, and she twisted her body and flipped Marc over, straddling his hips. She motioned for me to join them on the bed and I kneeled down beside her and kissed her on her lips. I could feel her body writhing over Marc's midsection, and I ran my hands down her stomach to feel their connection. Marc's hard cock was flat against his stomach as Heather rolled back and forth over it with her wet pussy. I played with her clit and she began to moan in my mouth.

Then she began lowering herself until our mouths were inches away from Marc's throbbing phallus. She swung her leg over to Marc's opposite side and his penis popped up into an acute sixty-degree angle, pointing toward his head. In the soft moonlight streaming through Heather's balcony doors, I could see that it was large, straight, and magnificent. The head glistened with a mixture of pre-cum and Heather's juices, and we both wrapped our fingers around it.

While we gave him a slow, two-handed massage, Marc sighed and thrust his manhood into our pliant hands. After a couple of minutes, Heather lowered her head and took him into her mouth, as I cupped his balls and played with the space between his testicles and anus. Marc moaned and began to roll his hips more aggressively, obviously enjoying Heather's attention on his cock. I could hear his passion rising and I began to feel his balls tighten and rise up. I knew it wouldn't take long for him to come with the combined effect of two beautiful women attending to his erogenous area.

Heather must have sensed it too because she lifted her head off his dick and leaned over and kissed me. Marc began to raise himself up wanting to get in on the action, but Heather extended her right hand and pushed him back onto the bed. He quickly got the message and watched the two of us while we explored each other's bodies. I cupped Heather's tits again and rolled her nipples between my fingers, then we pressed our chests together and tribbed our nipples while we fucked each other's mouths with our tongues.

By this time, all three of us were ready for some direct stimulation, and I hesitated, unsure where to go next. It was my first time in a threesome—at least one where I had this degree of control—and I didn't want to leave anyone hanging. Heather suddenly lifted her right leg and swung it over Marc's stomach, then did the same with her other leg until she was straddling his hips from the side. She motioned for me to do the same, then we pulled each other forward until our vulvas touched Marc's throbbing member on opposite sides. It was an incredible sensation feeling the heat of his hard cock sandwiched between our two pussies. Heather and I wasted no time moving our hips up and down, giving Marc an entirely new type of erotic massage.

The three of us were now getting direct stimulation, and Heather and I moaned in each other's mouths as we rubbed our soaking pussies together against Marc's pointed cock. I could feel our combined wetness running between my legs, as I pushed harder against Marc's warm and wonderful joystick. I wrapped my arms around Heather's waist and pulled her closer toward me. By now, we were all moaning in abandon and nearing the tipping point. I tilted my hips downward a bit and pressed my clit against the side of Marc's cock. Heather and I were humping him hard now, and our tits rubbed together as sweat streamed down our stomachs. This was an entirely new kind of tribbing that I'd never experienced before, and the image of the three of us joined together soon put me over the edge.

I threw my head back and let out a primal scream as Heather and I thrashed our hips together and gushed all over Marc's throbbing hard-on. We kissed for another minute as we came down from our high, then we separated and peered at Marc. He had a silly smile on his face, but his cock was still pointing up, bobbing gently over his stomach from the pulse flowing through its veins. I ran my hand over my stomach to see if I could detect any sign of semen on me, then I looked at Heather and shook my head to signal that he hadn't come yet.

"Good boy," she said, leaning over to give him a long, lingering kiss.

Then she shifted her body until her hips were behind his head, and she looked at me, silently nodding. I knew her intent immediately, and I swung my legs over Marc's midsection, straddling his hips in her direction. She lifted herself up, placing her pussy over his face, then lowered herself onto his eager mouth. I could see her eyes roll back in her head as he took her swollen clit between his lips and began to suck her, and she began to grind her hips into his face.

I didn't need any more encouragement. I grabbed Marc's thick schlong and directed the tip toward my quivering opening. I teased him for just a second, rubbing his sticky head against my clit and vulva, then I lowered myself onto him until his mound pressed firmly against my clit. As Heather and I locked eyes, I convulsed in a mini-orgasm.

It was an unbelievably hot sight watching each other fuck this adonis from opposite ends as we watched our passion rising. I began to rock my hips in unison with Heather, and I could feel Marc's hips answering the call. I loved the feeling of his big cock filling me up, and he knew how to move his hips to give my clit direct stimulation. The combined feeling of my clit grinding into his mound and the head of his cock rubbing against my G-spot was driving me crazy. I began moaning more loudly as I stepped up the pace of my humping action, while Heather and I clasped hands.

I wanted to make this last as long as I could, but the sights and sounds of three beautiful people joining together in an erotic union was too much. I could feel my orgasm welling deep inside me and I made one final push down hard onto Marc's cock as I squeezed Heather's hands like a vice. When I finally came, I grunted like a wild animal as my body spasmed over Marc's hips while I looked Heather straight in her eyes.

I guess that was too much for Marc too, because he grabbed my hips with two hands and thrust his hips into the air, lifting me off the mattress as I felt his cock throbbing in rhythmic contractions inside my pussy. With him moaning into her pussy and her seeing me have a powerful orgasm, it soon put Heather over the edge. Just as I was beginning to feel the last of my contractions subside, her hands squeezed mine hard and her eyelids narrowed as she clamped her thighs around Marc's head. She growled like a dog in heat as

I watched the pleasure roll over her pretty face. The whole time we never took our eyes off one another.

When she finally collected her breath and came down from her orgasm, she smiled at me. We were both thinking the same thing. My new partner in crime and I had found our first accomplice.

5

WATER SPORTS

Later that evening, Marc returned to his room and Heather and I continued to make love into the wee hours. By 3:00 a.m., we were both spent, and we fell asleep sprawled naked atop the bed sheets, as a cool breeze from the ocean wafted over our sweaty bodies. When the morning sun streamed through her balcony door, Heather rolled over and caressed my breast.

"Morning, Sunshine," she said, as my eyes slowly flitted open.

"Morning, Beautiful," I said, moving in closer to give her a kiss.

"That was quite a first night we had together."

"Mmmm, yes," I said, tasting her sweet tongue in my mouth. "Hopefully the first of many."

"I hope so too. But I don't want to steal all your time and attention on this cruise. The main idea is to mix it up and take advantage of as many activities as you can in the limited time you have available."

"Can't we do that together?" I asked.

"Some of them, for sure. But I think some of the other

activities you might enjoy more on your own."

"What about our new friend Marc?"

"I'm pretty sure he'll want to get out there on his own and sow some more of his oats. But he left his room number on my nightstand, so we might have a chance to hook up with him again before the cruise is over."

I looked out the open balcony doors at the sun shimmering over the open sea.

"You've done this before. What activity do you recommend we try next?"

"Most people like to ease into this whole nudity thing. Let's head up to the pool and do some people watching while we work on our tans. There's also a cool fountain on the top deck that's quite fun and refreshing. But first, I think we should get something to eat. I don't know about you, but I'm famished!"

"Me too. I think we burned enough calories last night for *three* meals. But first I'd like to return to my cabin to freshen up. What do you recommend I wear to breakfast?"

"It'll be pretty hot up top. A bikini and sandals should be enough. You'll just be taking it all off pretty soon anyway. You don't want to have to carry a bunch of clothes around with you."

"That reminds me," I suddenly remembered. "I've still got to retrieve my stuff from last night in the lounge."

"Something tells me you're not going to need jeans and a blouse for a while. We can pick that up on our return to our cabins later in the day. Did you want to borrow my shawl to get back to your room?"

I smiled at Heather's thoughtfulness.

"I'm just a few doors down. Judging by last night, half the people on the ship are already nude, so a little more streaking down the hall shouldn't hurt me."

"You're going to need a key to get in though. I'm guessing you didn't think of my trick."

Heather leaned over and picked up her room phone then tapped some numbers on the dial.

"Yes," she spoke into the phone, "my friend's lost her key for room E48. Can you send someone down with a replacement? She's in my room, E32. Thank you."

Ten minutes later, there was a soft tap on Heather's door.

"Maybe I'll take you up on that shawl offer after all," I said.

Heather smiled and went to her closet and held the garment open for me as I slid my arms into it.

"Meet you in the Poseidon Restaurant in an hour?" she said.

"Deal," I said, giving her a quick kiss.

I opened the door, gave Heather a playful shake of my ass, then followed the porter back to my room.

After breakfast, Heather led me to the main pool on the top deck, where scores of people were lounging naked on deck chairs and playing in the water. A series of interconnected pools simulated the look of a tropical lagoon, complete with life-size palm trees and small cabanas. We found a couple of open lounge chairs not far from the bar, and Heather asked me to mind them for us while she went to get a couple of drinks.

While she was gone, I made a quick scan of the scene. Virtually everybody was already naked, and it was a busy hive of activity. On one end of the lagoon, a large waterslide deposited screaming guests into the splashing water. In an adjacent basin, a small group of people were playing water polo. On the other side of the patio, a few passengers were skipping through a water fountain like a bunch of playful toddlers. It was all pretty surreal, and I paused to take it all in.

"Checking out all the action?" Heather said, returning from the bar and handing me a drink.

"Mmm, yes," I said, taking a sip of my pina colada. "There's certainly a lot of...*diversions*."

"Are you referring to all the naked people or the activities?"

"Both," I said, scanning the bodies of some of the men walking around the pool. "It's strange, though. Everybody seems so...*asexual*. I would have thought more people would be, you know, *aroused*, seeing each other naked."

"That's the thing about us all being in the same boat, so to speak. Like I said earlier, nudity is the great equalizer. Everybody gets used to it pretty quickly, and before you know it they're walking around like it's a normal walk in the park." Heather paused as she appraised my demeanor. "Are you disappointed?"

"Not really. I just expected the men in particular would be showing more sign of, you know, *interest*. The cruise operator billed this as more of a sex cruise than a nude cruise."

Heather smiled, as she lay back on her lounge chair.

"Believe me, there'll be plenty of opportunity for you to get down and dirty on this cruise. There's more going on than might first appear. For instance, take a look at that woman standing in the fountain on the other side of the patio."

I peered across the pool and saw a naked woman in her twenties standing over some jets of water spraying up from the surface. She had a strange look on her face as she spread her legs and squatted over the stream.

"It looks like she's having an enema," I laughed.

"I think she's directing the spray to a *different* part of her body," Heather said.

The look on the woman's face changed to one of pleasure as she began to shimmy her hips over the water stream. Suddenly the spray started pulsing like a shower head, and she let out a low moan.

I crossed my legs, beginning to feel a tingle in my pussy.

"I see what you mean," I said. "Now I see why they call it the Fantasy Fountain."

Heather noticed me squirming on my chair.

"Do you feel like giving it a try?"

"In a sec. Let me enjoy her experience first."

The woman suddenly grabbed her tits with her hands and pushed them up, as the spray from the patio surface gushed up over her abdomen and washed over her face. She was grunting and groaning now and moving her hips more rhythmically over the jet.

"Fuck, that's hot," I said.

"Kind of a nice way to cool off on a hot day like this."

"It looks like it might take the edge off in more ways than one."

Suddenly, the woman began screaming, as her body convulsed and her hips shook in rhythmic spasms. There was no doubt to us or any of the many other spectators that she had just enjoyed a powerful orgasm. When she staggered out of the fountain back toward her lounge chair, a small round of applause rose from around the pool.

"What do you think?" Heather said. "Are you up for it?"

"Now that I know I'm going to have an audience, I wouldn't mind some company. Will you come with me?"

"I think I will," Heather said, winking at me. "Let's toss these bikinis first. We don't want anything getting in the way of all the fun."

Heather nonchalantly unclasped her bikini top behind her back then stepped out of her bottoms. I'd almost forgotten how beautiful she was, and her tanned body looked magnificent in the bright sunshine. Her shaved pussy left nothing to the imagination, and I could see her nub poking out of her labia at the top of her pussy.

"Damn girl," I said, opening my eyes wide. "You're never afraid to let it all hang out."

"It's called a *fantasy cruise*, right? Let's live out our fantasies. Get those clothes off and let's go have some fun!"

I pulled off my top and bottom and threw them on my lounge chair, then Heather and I scampered around the pool past a throng of curious onlookers. When we got in the fountain, it was actually quite refreshing. The water was warm, but it felt cool against my hot skin in the blazing sun. The water jets were spread a few feet apart, facing different directions with alternating pulsing patterns. Some were a constant stream and some stopped and started periodically, while others pulsed at different speeds like an overhead shower faucet.

Heather and I stepped into the sprays and danced around for a minute, laughing and holding hands. Then we came together and kissed, rubbing our bodies together as the spray shot up between us, soaking our faces. Suddenly, I no longer cared about being naked in full view of the other pool guests. I was lost in the deluge of sensations I felt from the water jets spraying against my ass and Heather rubbing her body against mine.

We shifted position until we found a spot in the fountain where a steady stream directed toward our pussies. Then we pushed our mounds together so the stream sprayed directly against our touching clits. I opened my mouth and gasped as Heather smiled at me. This was a once-in-a-lifetime experience, and I wanted to enjoy every moment of it with her.

Suddenly, two more sprays began jetting at a forty-five-degree angle from behind each of us, and we bent our knees to give the spray direct access to our rosebuds.

"Oh my God!" I said to Heather, as my eyes flew open.

"Is this *arousing* enough for you?" she said, grinding her clit against mine.

"Fuck, yes!"

Just when I thought it couldn't get any more intense, the steady spray directed toward our clits began pulsing in strong, flickering streams.

"Uhnn," I moaned, closing my eyes at the intense feeling of pleasure I was experiencing from every part of my body.

"Enjoy, Baby," Heather said, as she thrust her tongue into my mouth, swaying her hips in tandem with mine.

I could feel the passion rising quickly inside me, and there was no way I could hold it back any longer.

"Fuck, I'm coming!" I said, as my pussy clenched inside me and I became weak in the knees. "Ohh, Ohh, Ohh," I panted into Heather's mouth, feeling the waves roll over me. Heather grunted into my mouth and I felt her hips shudder against mine as she reached her own peak. We moaned out loud together as the warm water from the jets sprayed all over our ecstatic faces.

When we finally came down from our orgasms, we held each other over the gentle spray, leaning against one another in exhaustion. When we separated, a loud cheer rose from around the pool from the appreciative crowd.

I guess this won't to be so hard getting used to after all, I thought.

6

PEAK SENSATIONS

Heather and I spent the rest of the day lounging around the pool, people watching. We made a few new friends and got some more cabin numbers, but mostly we just wanted to relax and scope out our next move. Heather said if we didn't pace ourselves, we'd either be too sore or exhausted to partake in some of the more adventurous shipboard activities. After perusing the ship's Fantasy Menu, we both agreed our next rendezvous would be at the climbing wall.

I went back to my cabin alone that night planning to get a good night's sleep, with visions of naked climbers exposing themselves as they scaled the cliff. I woke up refreshed the next morning, eager to try out the next erotic challenge. When I met Heather at the breakfast buffet, the room was filled with naked passengers filling their plates with hardly a sideways glance. I guess she'd been right about everybody getting comfortable being in the nude by the third day.

As she explained to me what to expect at the climbing

wall, my eyes widened in anticipation. It sounded terrifying and exciting at the same time.

"Do people ever *fall*?" I asked.

"Everyone's strapped into a harness and they have spotters to maintain tension on the rope holding you up, so even if you do slip, it's perfectly safe."

I frowned at the thought of other people watching my naked body from below.

"So I'll have some stranger watching my bare ass as I stretch my legs and move up the wall?"

"Yes, but that's part of the fun of it. Knowing other people are watching you as you get higher and higher is quite titillating, for both you and the observers. Plus, the staff doing the rope work are usually pretty buff, so it's kind of hot."

The idea of exposing my body while I stimulated myself on the wall reminded me of my Dinner Party experience. I squirmed in my seat reflecting back on the memory of Jasmine playing with me under the table while my fellow diners looked on.

"Tell me more about the unique 'features' on the wall."

"Besides the usual cup and lip-shaped ledges for gaining a comfortable hand and foot hold, there are other more *erotic* holds to clasp onto along the way."

"Such as?"

"For starters, some of the lips vibrate, so you can pause and get a little extra stimulation whenever you're feeling in the mood."

I pictured the idea of being in a harness clinging to a wall while sex toys stimulated my private parts.

"Now I see why they strap you in," I said. "I could barely maintain my balance on solid ground at the fountain yesterday, the more worked up I got. I can imagine how weak in the knees people might get, stimulated in a similar manner while climbing a challenging wall."

"Exactly," Heather said. "Especially the higher you go. The stimulation gets more and more intense the higher you climb."

"How so?"

"The features start out pretty tame at the bottom, just little nodules to rub against. But then they start vibrating, like little magic bullets. They get progressively larger and more animated the higher you go. If you make it all the way to the top, they've got some full-size dildos that twist and rotate to really give you a ride."

"Mmm," I said, feeling the moisture beginning to build inside my pussy. "Just like my favorite rabbit vibrator."

"Kind of like that. Except this time, you're suspended twenty-five feet off the ground in full view of your spotter and any other spectators while you get off."

Suddenly I had a burning need to have something inside me.

"That sounds pretty hot."

Heather raised her eyebrows and nodded.

"There's something about the whole idea that's very arousing. I think you'll find it's quite a different experience."

I wrinkled my forehead as I pondered the possibilities.

"What about the guys? Are there similar erotic features for *them* to enjoy on the wall?"

"Definitely. The wall holds alternate between 'innies' and 'outies', so everybody has a chance to enjoy. Many of them are fashioned in the form of flexible lips, pussies, and anuses, where men can insert their dongs along the way and get a similar thrill. Near the top, they become animated with internal vibrators, just like the bullets and dildos for the ladies. It's quite arousing to watch the men and women stop and fuck the life-like features along the way."

I shook my head and grimaced at a new thought.

"What about all the...*by-products* deposited along the way? It must get pretty slippery and gross before long. I wouldn't want to place my hands or my pussy anywhere near some dude's day-old cum."

Heather scrunched her nose and laughed.

"Not to worry. The ship operators have got it all figured out. After every new climber comes down from the wall, they cover the wall in a tarp and wash it down with high-powered steam water jets. They keep it all very antiseptic."

I clenched my legs together, trying to stimulate my burning clit. I couldn't wait to give it a try.

"What do you say?" Heather said. "Are you up for it?"

"Definitely. My pussy's ready to climb on just about anything right now!"

W hen we got to the wall, I was surprised by how tall it was. It towered at least thirty feet straight up, with foot and hand holds separated a few feet apart. It was odd but strangely arousing to see the artificial vulvas and dildos sticking out from its surface. Two naked people were already strapped into hip harnesses at the base of the wall, a man and a woman both appearing to be in their mid-20s.

They spoke with familiarity to one another, so I assumed they were a couple. What a thrill I thought it must be for the pair to experience this together. A small crowd of friends and onlookers were gathered a few feet further back from the wall, egging the couple on. As Heather had described, two buff staff members held thick ropes in their hands, which looped up over an extended wheel at the top of the structure. The other end dangled down the front of the facade and clasped securely to the front of their harnesses.

"Are you ready?" the man said, looking at his partner.

She nodded silently, then reached up for the first handhold and placed her foot onto a lip at the base of the wall. Heather looked at me and smiled. The idea of doing this in tandem appealed to me, and I hoped that the two of us would have our turn soon. It was strange watching the climbers spread their legs and bend their asses as they stretched to reach the next higher holds. I could see the man's balls hanging between his thighs and his penis wobbling back and forth as he swung from one placement to the other. They both seemed so focused on figuring out their path of ascent that they barely paused to rest.

But about half way up, the woman suddenly paused and pushed her hips against the wall. I could see a small ball-shaped object resting between her thighs, nestled against her vulva. A gentle vibrating noise emanated from the area. She looked over at her partner and smiled, encouraging him to find a similar place to rest. He glanced to his left and saw an orange ring protruding from the wall. He stepped up and over until his cock was level with the ring then he positioned his flaccid member inside the hole. Suddenly the ring started vibrating, and the man threw his head back. I could see his cock hardening and lengthening as he positioned the vibrating ring around the glans of his penis. He turned toward his partner and they giggled while they gently humped the wall together.

"Higher! Higher!" their friends urged them on from the bottom of the wall.

The two reluctantly disengaged from their fixed positions and resumed their climb up the wall. About five feet higher up, the woman came upon a curved rubber dildo protruding about three inches from the surface, and she paused over it then lowered her pussy until it disappeared inside her hole. She started humping the small dildo to cheers from the crowd. I was glad everybody's attention was focused on the wall, because my fingers had already begun circling my clit as I matched the woman's hip movements.

The man noticed a new feature on his side of the wall, this time mimicking the lips and tongue of a woman. He didn't hesitate to slip his now fully erect cock inside the orifice and begin to moan as he deep-throated his artificial lover. Both he and his partner began speeding up the movement of their hips and it looked like one or both of them might come soon. But the crowd at the base of the wall weren't quite ready.

"Get to the pussy and the dick at the top!" someone shouted. "You're almost there!"

The couple glanced at one another then looked down and shook their heads in mock frustration. Then they peered up the wall and resumed their climb. All the while, the two staff members holding the ropes held the lines taut while pretending to be uninterested in the actions of the climbers. But I noticed the telltale bulge in their pants that belied their disinterest. I looked over at Heather and saw that her hand had slipped between her legs too.

The couple picked up their climbing speed with new determination, and it didn't take long for them to near the top of the wall, where the woman was presented with a large purple dildo and the man with a gaping artificial pussy. The woman placed her lips around the dildo and pretended to give it blowjob while the man pushed his face into the artificial vulva and shook his head playfully. The crowd below erupted in a loud cheer.

"Fuck it! Fuck it! Fuck it!" they chanted in unison.

The woman climbed a few feet higher, then placed the big dildo inside her pussy, and relaxed her legs. The staff member holding her rope bent his knees, clasping the end of the rope tightly with two hands. He'd obviously been in this situation before, and he braced himself for the shifting load. Just a few feet away on the other side of the wall, the man positioned himself adjacent to the artificial vulva and inserted his dick into the hole.

"Whomp! Whomp! Whomp!" chanted their friends down below, in encouragement.

With everybody's attention focused on the wall, Heather suddenly moved behind me and squeezed my breast with one hand, while she slipped her fingers inside my cunny from behind. I could hear vibrating sounds emanating from the artificial pussy and dildo, and the man and the woman clenched their buttocks as they began to fuck their sex toys more vigorously. They peered over at one another and mouthed something, and I could hear their breathing escalating in urgency.

Heather began to speed up the pace of her ministrations, and I fucked her fingers as I pretended it was me on the wall. Within a minute or so, the couple's bodies began convulsing, and their arms and legs suddenly became rigid. Heather held me tightly while I clamped down hard on her hand as I came at the same time with the couple on the wall.

The handlers held the couple's lines firmly until they pushed away from the edifice and were gently lowered. When they got to the bottom and removed their harnesses, their friends surrounded them in a group hug, jumping up and down in celebration. The staff ordered everybody to step ten feet back from the wall, then a canvas tarp descended from the top and hot jets began cleaning the surface. I could feel the steam rising above the tarp as a rivulet of water began pooling at the base of the structure, draining into a grated hole beside the podium.

I turned around and looked at Heather. She raised her eyebrows to signal if I was game to try it next. I simply nodded my head and smiled. I could feel my own rivulet of warm liquid running down my legs.

7

HOUSE OF HOLES

After they finished sanitizing the wall, Heather and I took our turn on it. Most of the spectators had moved on after the previous couple came down, but it was still unnerving being watched so closely by our rope handlers. As usual, Heather took the lead sitting over the erotic extrusions, and the look of delight on her face soon encouraged me to do the same. We came multiple times grinding our pussies into the various devices, culminating with two powerful orgasms on the large dildos at the top of the wall.

We spent a few more hours lounging around the pool, then Heather encouraged me to strike out on my own. I protested briefly, still not entirely comfortable with the idea of engaging in public sex by myself, but she suggested a few venues that might provide an opportunity for more privacy. After a quick lunch, I reluctantly began exploring the ship.

My first stop was the Sexy Games Room. It was filled with various contraptions, where solo men and women were getting fucked by automated machines. At one station, a woman bent over on all fours, while a large plastic dildo pounded in and out of her pussy. At another one, a man sat on a chair humping a life-like silicone doll, while he squeezed her fake tits and thrust his tongue into her fellatio-shaped mouth. In the corner of the room, a pretty co-ed straddled a device that looked like a pommel horse, as she bucked and writhed atop its vibrating saddle.

It all seemed so surreal and impersonal for me. I wanted a *human* connection, like the one Heather and I shared at the fantasy fountain. I scanned the activity menu and considered going for an Intimate Massage, thinking at least this way I'd have some human touch, and then I remembered one of Heather's recommendations. The description for the House of Holes sounded intriguing:

Hook up with a stranger on the other side of a wall through your own personal intimate portal. You can choose to 'give', 'receive', or 'merge' with a partner of either sex in an erotic and completely anonymous connection. Or you can choose to simply watch, as other couples get their groove on in this sensuous and erotic 'House of Holes'.

Yes, I thought, *'merging' with a partner is exactly what I need.* The notion of engaging with someone through my own personal 'glory hole', reminded me of the fun I'd had playing with hidden strangers in the Dark Room.

When I got to the venue and opened the door, the first thing I noticed was the sound. A cacophony of moans and grunts greeted me, as a variety of naked men and women shimmied their hips, asses, and mouths against the vinyl-coated walls. The lights were dimmed, but I could see the unmistakable shape of erect penises and vulvas poking through various small holes scattered around the room.

People on the other side were shaking their hips trying

to get the attention of someone from inside the room, but everybody was already engaged in some form of coupling. One man was humping the wall, being serviced by someone from the other side. Another one kneeled on the floor giving head to a well-endowed fellow who thrust his cock vigorously into his consort's eager mouth. Not far away, a woman bent over rubbing her ass against the wall, where another man plunged his cock through the hole into her pussy.

But the whole scene somehow left me cold. It struck me as cheap and dirty. Medical clearance or not, I couldn't get on board with the idea of connecting with some other stranger's private parts in such an impersonal way. Just as I was about to leave the room, I noticed a neon sign in the corner reading 'Private View Rooms'.

Private definitely sounded more appealing. And being able to *see* my partner was more along my lines.

I opened the door and entered a dimmed hall with closed doors lining both sides. Most of them were locked with a sign reading 'Occupied', but a little further down the hall I found one marked 'Vacant'. I turned the handle and stepped into a small room. It had a single vinyl chair facing a floor-to-ceiling glass wall with a one-foot diameter hole cut in the middle. On the other side of the glass was a similar room with an empty chair.

I turned and locked my door, then checked the chair to see if it was clean. There were no visible marks or residue, but I ran my hand over its smooth surface just to be sure. Even the vinyl floor looked like it had just been cleaned, reflecting the light from the single overhead incandescent lamp.

At least they clean up after themselves pretty well, I nodded, as I sat down on the chair and waited for someone to enter the adjacent room.

I expected a man looking for a simulated adult video store glory hole experience, but I was pleasantly surprised when a slim young Asian girl opened the door. She paused for a moment and appraised me seated in my chair with my legs slightly ajar, then she turned around and locked her door from the inside. She was carrying something but she kept it hidden from my view as she turned around.

We could have easily talked if we'd wanted to, with a large enough hole in the glass to carry on a private conversation. But we both seemed to want to just *look* for the time being. She sat down on her chair and placed the hidden object behind her, then spread her legs apart. She had a petite figure with firm B-cup breasts and a small V-shaped patch of pubic hair on her mound that pointed toward a protruding nub at the top of her labia. She had large eyes with long lashes, and she smiled at me as she began to run her hands over her body.

I watched her for a moment, as I felt the juices from my pussy puddle on the chair in front of me. She placed her hands on the inside of her thighs and pulled them slowly toward her apex, then continued moving them up toward her chest. She squeezed her tits then pushed them up and tilted her head down, sucking each of her nipples.

I wanted a piece of her so badly, but I was enjoying her little striptease. I cupped my left breast with one hand and I began to play with my clit with my other, spreading my legs further apart. She did the same and pointed her toes, as she opened her mouth, signaling her pleasure. I could hear a soft moan emanating through the hole in the glass as she flitted her eyes and began to rock her hips on her chair.

By now I was thoroughly soaked, feeling the intensity rising in my loins. I slipped the fingers from my other hand into my pussy as I rubbed my clit more forcefully. The Asian girl suddenly thrust both of her hands into her love box and began fucking herself with a two-handed motion, rocking her chest in tandem with her hips. The sound of her juices sloshing around as she finger-fucked herself with both hands ratcheted my excitement up another level.

I could feel my orgasm beginning to build as I let out a low moan. The girl spread her legs wider until they were virtually straight out to her sides. I marveled at her flexibility, reminding me of my naked yoga experience with Kayla and Neve. We were groaning in tandem as we each fucked our own pussies, alternating our line of sight between our sopping pussies and our glazed-over eyes. Suddenly the girl's chest began to heave, and she grunted a staccato burst of moans as she hunched over in orgasmic spasms. That was enough to put me over the edge, and I growled like a wild animal as I gushed all over the chair in front of me. It was incredibly erotic watching each other come with only a few feet separating us between the clear pane of glass.

But now I was ready for a more personal connection. After I came down from my high, I stood up and walked toward the glass and motioned for her to do the same. She walked slowly toward the hole in the partition, then placed her palms flat against the glass at shoulder height. She was even prettier up close, with big brown eyes, high cheekbones, and full pouty lips. I placed my hands over hers and we moved our faces toward the glass until our lips touched on the cool surface. There was something about being this close to another naked woman and not being able to touch her that I found highly arousing.

Our opposite hands traced a path down the side of the glass and we reached through the hole to touch each other's pussies. I groaned when I felt the heat of her box and her fingers touching my clit. We lowered our bodies a few more inches to gain better access to our midsections while still peering into one another's eyes. I stuck out my tongue and began to lick the glass, showing that I was ready for a more personal touch.

I bent my knees a little further and her fingers slipped out of me as I squatted down over the hole in front of her pussy. She pushed her hips into the glass to try to give me better access, but it felt awkward tilting my head through the hole trying to get to her clit with my tongue. Sensing my frustration, she suddenly stepped back from the glass then lifted her right leg straight up and placed her heel against the glass beside her shoulder. Then she pushed her body forward until her legs were pressed flat against the glass in a perfect split.

Her open vulva was now pushing through the hole directly toward my face. I didn't hesitate to take her little button into my mouth and roll it around my tongue like a peppermint candy. Her lubrication coated my face as she ground her pussy against my cheeks. I reached through the hole and wrapped my arm around her hips, pulling her harder toward me. She moaned softly and whimpered as she fucked my face. I inserted two fingers into her love canal as I sucked and flicked her little cocklet in my mouth. Then I curled my fingers in a come-hither motion against her G-spot and she bent her knees, pressing her pussy harder against my face and fingers. Her moans were growing in intensity and my heart raced at the idea of her coming on my face. I pushed my fingers deeper inside and circled her clit more quickly with my tongue. Suddenly, she howled as her pussy clamped over my fingers in a long series of hard contractions. I held my face still while she gushed all over me.

If I could have squeezed my whole body through the

narrow opening in the glass, I would have pounced on her right then and there and tribbed her hard until we both came together. Instead, I slowly raised myself up until my face was at the same level as hers and kissed her gently against the glass. She smiled at me and blinked twice as if to say 'thank you'. Then she turned around and walked toward the chair and picked up the object which she'd gone to such pains to hide from me. She held it up in the dim light and smiled. It was a long two-sided flexible dildo, anatomically correct on both ends, shaped like a two-headed penis.

Fuck, yes, I thought. *That's what I'm talking about.*

I wanted to fuck this girl so badly, and the two-sided dildo was just what the doctor ordered. She walked up to the glass and held it up in front of me, then licked it up and down the shaft. Then she placed one end in her mouth and simulated fellatio over the silicone glans.

Please, I mouthed through the glass. *I need it inside of me now.*

Demonstrating my urgency, I turned around and placed my ass against the open hole, then bent over to present my open pussy to her. She pushed the dildo through the hole and rubbed it back and forth across my vulva, and I shuddered in pleasure. I bucked my hips against the phallus and pressed my ass harder against the glass, signaling that I wanted her to place it inside me.

When she finally did, I almost fainted in pleasure. The feeling of the thick dildo pushing inside me from behind was exquisite. She pushed it as far as it would go, then I felt some slack on the device as she turned around and faced her ass toward me. I didn't need to look to know what she was doing, as I felt the pressure of the dildo when she pushed the other end inside her own pussy.

When our buttocks touched through the open glass, we

groaned as we began to simultaneously fuck the giant phallus. I could feel her juices coating the dildo on the other end as our pussies sloshed and bucked against our imaginary partner. The girl began to whimper as we ground our asses together, trying to come over the thick joystick between our legs. It didn't take long for us to reach our peak as we screamed and shook in simultaneous orgasms on the writhing snake embedded inside us.

It took us over a minute before we were ready to disengage, when the girl finally separated herself from the two-headed dildo and pulled it out of my throbbing pussy. I turned around and placed my lips against the glass, and we kissed one last time before she silently picked up the dildo and exited the room. No words had been necessary the entire time we shared our intimate connection.

Just as I was turning to leave, a buff young man entered the room the girl had just left. I took one look at his large swinging cock and shook my head.

I wouldn't mind a taste of the real thing, I thought.

8

STRAIGHT FLUSH

After I had another go with my new partner in the private view room, I staggered back to my room, sore and exhausted. I slept like a log that night, dreaming of animated cocks and pussies attached to life-like trees, as I walked through a magical forest. When I woke up in the morning, I lay in a giant wet spot atop my leaking cunny and rubbed another one out before showering and heading upstairs to meet Heather for breakfast.

She laughed when I told her about my strange dream, and we entertained each other over lox and pineapple with stories of our experiences from the previous day. She seemed interested in my private view room encounter, but when I told her about my disappointment with the games room, her ears perked up.

"You didn't explore the *other* games rooms?" she said.

"What other games rooms? I only found the one with the holes in the wall."

"There are lots of others that you might find interesting. One of my favorites is the Card Lounge."

"What happens there?"

"It's where groups of people meet to play card games."

"That doesn't sound very interesting."

"It *is* when everybody's naked and they play by different rules."

Heather noticed Marc heading back from the buffet and motioned for him to join them. Virtually everybody was now walking around the ship completely naked, paying little mind to the jiggling breasts and penises as people went about their daily routines.

"Good morning, ladies," Marc said, as he approached our table. "How have you found your shipboard experience so far?"

I took a good long look at Marc's body before he sat down, refreshing my memory from our first night together. Standing well over six feet tall, his well-muscled torso and arms rippled in the bright light streaming through the windows on the top deck. His penis was flaccid, but still hanging a healthy five to six inches as it swung gently above his nicely shaved balls. I picked a thick piece of pineapple from my plate, remembering what his dick felt like standing straight up.

"I think the word is...*eclectic*," I said, sucking the dripping fruit between my lips.

Marc sat down quickly on the other side of our booth to hide his growing erection and smiled.

"There's certainly no shortage of diversions," he said, scooping a large forkful of scrambled eggs into his mouth. "Have you had a favorite experience?"

"You mean besides our little tryst with you?" Heather said, grabbing a sausage from his plate and biting it in half.

"Of course I knew that would be your highlight," Marc said, continued the tease. "I was referring to the venues."

"The climbing wall was fun," Heather said. "But I think

Jade may have experienced a different kind of high in one of the private view rooms yesterday."

"Oh? You like those sexy holes, do you?"

"Some holes were a little sexier than others," I said.

"Jade found the rest of the games room a bit under-whelming. I was suggesting she try her hand at a little strip poker. Care to join us after breakfast?"

"Just the three of us?" Marc said.

"I think we need a plus-one to balance things out. Maybe we can persuade one of the guys from the House of Holes to take his dick out of the wall and find a more interesting use for it."

Marc stretched his lips and nodded.

"Game on," he said, finishing his sausage and eggs.

W hen we got to the card room, we saw an empty round glass table with a pack of playing cards and four trays of betting chips. Heather excused herself for a moment, then returned a few minutes later holding a college-age boy's hand. He looked a little perplexed as he stared at the three of us and the empty table.

"*Three's* a lot more fun than one, don't you think?" she said to the young man. "Plus, there's no barriers here to limit your engagement. Are you ready to play some sexy games?"

He paused for a moment, then stuck out his hand.

"I'm Liam," he said, signaling his assent.

After we all introduced ourselves, we took alternating seats at the table and Heather cracked open the pack of cards.

"What are we playing?" Liam enquired.

"Five card stud," Heather said, winking at me. "With two *real* studs. You *do* know how to play poker, Liam?"

"Yes, but what are the stakes? I didn't bring any money..."

"You're so cute," Heather said. "We're not playing for money. We're playing for *favors*. The rule is that whoever wins each hand, gets to command one or more of us to perform some kind of act. Whoever ends up with the most chips at the end of the hour gets to propose a special group activity. The only limitation is that no one is allowed to come until the very end."

"That makes it a little more interesting," Marc said.

"And challenging," Liam said, crossing his legs to hide his growing erection under the table.

"Right then," Heather said, pulling two red chips from her tray. "The ante is ten dinars."

"Dinars?" Liam said.

"It's just *play* money, remember? They gain *real* value a little later."

Heather dealt one card face down to each player then one more face up. We each looked at our hole cards and placed our bets. Liam placed the largest stake in the pile, then Heather dealt another set of cards face up. Liam showed two Kings and threw in one of his three black chips.

"Too steep for me," Marc huffed, pushing his cards into the waste pile.

Heather displayed two tens, and I had a Jack-high.

Heather matched Liam's bet, and I decided to fold. She dealt the fourth card to herself and Liam. Heather got a Queen, while Liam showed an Ace.

"Hooo!" Marc cheered, as he rubbed his hands together. "Now it's getting interesting. Think hard about what you want the ladies to do for you, Liam."

"I'm *already* hard," Liam said.

I looked through the table top between his legs and saw his good-sized cock pointing straight up on his belly.

Marc reached into his tray and tossed another black marker on the table. Heather paused trying to read his face, then she glanced beneath the table at his throbbing cock.

"I think he's bluffing," she said. "I'll match your bet and raise you one hundred." She threw down her last two black chips then dealt the last card face up. She got another ten and Liam got a six.

Liam didn't hesitate to throw his last black chip in the pot.

"I call," he said, then he turned over his hole card and revealed three Kings.

"Whoa," Heather said, opening her eyes wide in surprise. She turned over her card and revealed a two. Liam had won the hand.

"Well played, young man," Heather said. "Your wish is our command. What would you like us to do?"

Liam ran his eyes up and down Heather's figure and smiled.

"I want you to spread your legs and play with yourself."

Heather pushed her chair back from the table to give everyone a commanding view of her crotch, then she spread her legs apart. She began to circle her clit, while she stared Liam directly in the eyes. His breathing increased as his gaze wandered between her legs. She began to move her hips on the chair, and Liam's hand dropped down to his lap where he began rubbing his cock.

"Hey!" Heather admonished. "That's not allowed. You get to watch only."

"But you said as long as we don't cum—"

"There'll be plenty of time for that later. I want you boys to save those nice big hard-ons for the main event."

Heather sat back up and handed the remaining pack of cards to Liam.

"Your turn to deal," she said.

"That's it?" Liam said. "That was hardly worth three hundred dinars!"

Heather placed her moist fingers in her mouth and licked off her juices.

"You better play your hand wisely the rest of the way, then. Now you've got some extra cash to up the ante. We're just getting started."

Liam collected the pot from the middle of the table, then we all threw in two blue chips for the next round. Liam dealt the cards, and I won the next round with a full house.

I looked at Marc and Liam and licked my lips. I noticed that Liam's dick had lost some of its firmness, but Marc's was rapidly elongating under the table. I wondered how far he'd be willing to go with this game.

"I want Liam to suck Marc's cock," I said.

"What?" Liam said, his eyes flying open. "But I'm not...*gay*."

"It's just a game," Heather said. "No one's going to cum in your mouth, right Marc? At least not yet. Besides, how do you know if you don't like it until you try? Now get down there and suck that bratwurst."

Marc swung his chair out, and I noticed his cock was standing at full mast. Apparently at least *one* of the boys liked the idea of sucking another guy. Liam walked around the table and kneeled down in front of Marc. He stared at the tip of Marc's manhood, unsure what to do.

"Go on," Heather said. "It won't bite you. Just think of it as a popsicle. A very large warm popsicle."

Marc pulled his arms around behind his chair and clasped his hands together to give Liam freer access.

Liam opened his mouth and slowly lowered himself over the head of Marc's joystick. At first he just held it there, but after a few seconds he began to bob his head as Marc slowly swung his hips. They both seemed to be enjoying it, and I had to fight hard to keep my hands away from my steaming pussy. The sight of seeing two hetero men going at it was incredibly erotic. I wanted to see if I could push it a little further.

"Now play with his balls," I ordered.

Liam paused and peered up at me out of the corner of his eyes, and I simply nodded. Marc pushed his hips toward the end of his seat until his tight balls poked over the edge. Liam reached up and cupped them then rolled them gently between his fingers. His own cock had resumed its full length and was bobbing against his flat stomach. It was obvious that he was getting turned on by the experience, and I saw his tongue begin to roll around in his mouth as he circled the head of Marc's cock. Marc let out a groan and lifted his hips higher. I would have happily forfeited the game at that moment to watch Marc cum in Liam's mouth, but Heather interjected to remind us of the rules.

"Okay, I think that's enough for this round," she said. "You boys seem to be having a little bit too much fun."

Liam sheepishly disengaged from Marc and returned to his seat at the other side of the table. We resumed the game, with each round ratcheted up the degree of engagement between the players. Marc won the next round and asked Heather to sit in my lap while we tribbed each other for a couple of minutes. Then Heather won the next round and asked the men to do the same as we watched them jack their two cocks together between their bellies. By the time our hour was up, all four of us were worked up enough to jump each other bones. When we counted our chips, Heather had eked out Liam for the largest residual.

"What now?" Liam said, his cock bobbing on his stomach, already leaking pre-cum.

"I ended up with the highest winnings," Heather said, "so I get to decide on the final group activity. And I think we should all come back to my cabin."

We didn't bother to clean up the table as we quickly found the nearest exit. Unlike our first night together when we'd scurried down the stairs to her stateroom, this time we took the elevator down the three levels to her floor. But the tension in the lift was palpable as none of us said a word to one another, holding our collective breath in anticipation of what would come next.

9

FOUR PLAY

When we got to Heather's room, nobody was sure who should make the first move. When it was just the three of us, Heather hadn't hesitated to jump the only man in the room, but this time we had to figure out what to do with Liam. The obvious thing would have been for us to pair up as two hetero couples, but Heather had seen enough in the games room to have other ideas.

"You boys lie down on the bed with your feet facing each other," she ordered.

Marc and Liam dutifully lay on the mattress as Heather instructed.

"Now bend your knees and move together until your cock and balls are touching one another."

I looked at Heather inquisitively, wondering what she had planned. We'd already seen the men frotting their cocks together in the games room, and I was eager for some of my own touching.

She glanced at Marc and Liam's glistening cocks throbbing against each other and smiled at me.

"Do you want to go first or me?"

I pinched my eyebrows for a second, then gasped when I understood her intention. The idea of having two cocks inside me was something I hadn't yet experienced. I moved toward the bed and kneeled on the mattress straddling the two men, facing Liam. I'd already watched Marc come inside me, this time I wanted to picture a younger man's reaction.

The men paused for a moment, unsure what I wanted. They were probably thinking of the classic DP maneuver, where one would fuck me in my pussy while the other fucked me up the ass. But I had a better idea. Ever since I saw them rubbing their cocks together in the game room, I'd fantasized about grasping them both inside my pussy. Both men were well hung, measuring together at least three times the girth of an average man's erect penis, but I figured if my anatomy could accommodate a baby's head during childbirth, surely it could take the equivalent of two good sized English cucumbers.

I reached around behind my ass and clasped their two penises together then slowly lowered my pussy until it touched the wet heads of their joined hard-ons. Marc's was a little bit longer, so it pushed its way through first, as I felt my lips widen to accommodate his large organ. Slowly sitting down another inch, I could feel Liam's cockhead pressing me apart still further, and I moaned as I felt my pussy stretch to take them both inside me. With both of them lying flat on their backs on the mattress, there was little they could do with the full weight of my body pressing down over their hips. I relished the feeling of control, watching Liam's face contorting in pleasure as my love tunnel squeezed over their joined cocks.

I slowly lowered myself until I felt my vulva resting on

Liam's stubbly pubis. I was glad I'd placed Marc in the posterior position, where he had a little more room to sheath his larger cock. I began to use my thigh muscles to move up and down over their connected meat and reflected back on the Asian girl's two-headed cock from the view room the previous day. Two double pricks in as many days was a new milestone for me.

It seemed as if every nook and crevice of my pussy was filled up by the hot, throbbing manhood of these two virile men. I humped them faster, knowing it wouldn't to take long for all of us to come after the long buildup in the game room. Before long, Heather decided she wanted a piece of the action, and I could hear Marc's muffled moans behind me as she sat over his face. The look on Liam's face was priceless. I wasn't sure which he was enjoying more—the feeling of having his cock deeply embedded in my wet pussy, or the feeling of having Marc's throbbing member next to his.

His mouth was wide open as he moaned loudly in pleasure, and I knew he wouldn't be long to this world. I placed my hands over his tight pecs and squeezed the two-headed python inside me as I felt a powerful urge welling inside me. Heather suddenly reached around my back and squeezed my tits and we all howled in unison. When I came, I bucked wildly over the two men as I felt their cocks pulsing together, flooding me inside with their honey.

I sat there for a minute savoring the feeling of having two hard dicks inside me, as I peered out Heather's balcony window at the sun setting over the ocean. This cruise had been one hell of an adventure, and I didn't know if or when I'd have another chance like this again. I wanted to make it last as long as possible.

THE
SUBWAY
AFFAIR
AN EROTIC ADVENTURE
VICTORIA RUSH

Everyone's an exhibitionist in disguise...

GIRLS' CAMP

AN EROTIC ADVENTURE

VICTORIA RUSH

Getting wet was never this much fun...

There's only one place you can live out your wildest fantasies...

Jade's EROTIC ADVENTURES

BOOKS 1 - 5

VICTORIA ROSE

The complete five-book bestselling series — 60% off

THE SUBWAY AFFAIR - PREVIEW

DRESS UP

That night I could hardly sleep. I couldn't stop thinking about what had happened on the subway. I came three more times visualizing the memory of the brunette fingering me on the crowded train. It wasn't just the idea of having public sex that turned me on, it was the danger of the act that brought it to a new level. If either of us had been caught, we could have been charged with indecent behavior and led out of the station in handcuffs. When I finally did nod off, I dreamt of being fondled by multiple strangers, surrounded by oblivious travelers focused on other distractions.

I woke up with a giant wet spot on the sheets and staggered to the shower to get ready in time for day two of my conference. I figured the previous day's encounter was a once-in-a-lifetime fluke, where I just happened to find myself next to someone bold enough to make such a brazen public advance. But I planned to be ready just in case. I wore a loose-fitting summer dress with no bra or panties, and three-inch platform sandals to provide easier access to my undercarriage. This time, there'd be no need to rush back to my hotel to change my soiled undergarments. Even if I wasn't able to hook up with the pretty brunette again, just the sensation of feeling the swirling air from the moving train on my bare pussy would be a thrill.

I knew it was a longshot that I'd find the brunette in the same place on the same train on two consecutive days. But she looked like a regular commuter, and I figured that if I timed it right, I might get lucky. I glanced at my watch and noticed that it was 7:30. I grabbed my purse and rushed out of my hotel room, already feeling the moisture building between my legs.

When I got to the subway station, I slipped my Metro-Card through the card reader then paused to get my bearings. I remembered turning to the right yesterday after passing through the turnstiles to get away from the crowd, but I couldn't recall how far down the platform I'd gone before getting on the train. Then I noticed a familiar advertisement on the side wall. I walked toward it, then stepped forward to get closer to the edge of the platform. I didn't want to risk missing my train twice in as many days.

After a few minutes, a train rattled into the station and I swiveled my head trying to catch sight of the pretty brunette in one of the passing cars. But it was moving too fast and the cars were too full to make out any familiar faces. When the train came to a halt, I scanned inside the adjacent car, but I didn't see the brunette. I hesitated, unsure whether to enter the compartment.

Had I missed her train? I thought. *Was I too early, or too late? Should I wait for the next one to see if I can find her on that one?*

I searched frantically through the window at the south end of the carriage, but it was too densely packed with passengers to make anything out. Thinking she'd taken another seat out of view, I stepped into the car just before the door closed. As the train sped out of the station, I pushed my way through the crowd toward the end wall. When I got to the far corner, I was disappointed to see no sign of the brunette. I squeezed toward the window and grabbed hold of the overhead support bar. To my surprise, the same college girl who'd been standing behind me yesterday was seated on the bench in front of me, reading a book.

I craned my head toward the other end of the cabin to look for any sign of the brunette. Just when I was beginning to despair about ever seeing her again, a familiar scent tickled my nose.

That perfume! Could it be—.

I glanced in the window reflection and saw the brunette pushing her way through the crowd in my direction. She was a creature of habit, after all. Or maybe she just had the same idea I had—that if she got on the same train at the same time in the same place, she might be lucky enough to find that special someone who shared her predilection for public sex.

When she came up beside me, she took a similar position just to my left and behind me. Then she reached up and placed her hand over mine on the overhead bar and smiled at me in the window. She ran her eyes up and down my body, noticing my change of clothes and nodded with approval. Then she pressed in closer behind me and I felt her hand reach under my dress and squeeze my butt cheek. My ass trembled in excitement at her touch, and I spread my legs as far as I could to give her more space to reach between my legs.

She wasted no time plunging three fingers into my aching snatch, and I gasped out loud in pleasure. The college girl glanced up from her book and I coughed into my hand to distract her attention. The brunette paused until everybody's attention returned to their reading material, then she resumed finger-fucking me. I leaned over to tilt my pussy in her direction and noticed the college girl was no longer peering down at her book. Her eyelashes were fluttering just under her brow as she stared straight ahead at my dress. I wasn't sure if she'd noticed the brunette's hand movement under my garment, or if she merely suspected what was going on. Either way, I began to get worried and stopped moving my hips while I stared into the brunette's eyes in the window, trying to signal for her to stop before we got caught.

Fortunately, the train roared into the next station providing a temporary diversion. As it began to spit out passengers and take on a fresh load, the brunette pulled her fingers out of my pussy and began circling my clit. She was enjoying watching me squirm, and she had no intention of stopping her little tease. I closed my eyes and bit my lip as the new crop of passengers squeezed and pushed in behind us.

I noticed the college girl hadn't gotten off at the same stop as yesterday and saw that she was still peering straight ahead in the direction of my dress. I looked up at the brunette, pleading for her to stop until the train left the station. At least in the relative privacy of the darkened tunnel, the increased noise and jostling of the train would provide a temporary distraction from prying eyes. I wasn't sure if the brunette had also noticed the college girl's diverted attention. She simply smiled at me in the window as if to say: *So what if someone notices? Live in the moment, and revel in the extra attention.*

When the train finally sped out of the station, I glanced

at the subway map over the window and saw that our next stop was 86th Street. We wouldn't have long to finish our business before the next interruption. Sensing my concern, the brunette thrust her thumb into my pussy and began massaging my clit with the cup of her hand. I groaned softly and twisted my face in pleasure as she watched my tortured agony in the window.

I had to fight the temptation not to rock my hips, and I pushed down on her hand so she could fuck me deeper with her thumb. I was gushing all over her, and I was worried that someone might hear the suspicious sloshing sound emanating from between my legs. But the train must have been running behind schedule, and the sound of it racing through the noisy tunnel overpowered every other sound in the compartment.

I glanced down at the college girl and saw that she'd placed her book on her lap, cradling it open with two hands under its spine. Her knees were slightly parted, and her right hand was moving slowly under the book.

She was touching herself while she watched the brunette finger me under my dress!

The image of the girl rubbing herself while I was being fucked from behind sent a jolt through my body, and I felt my pleasure suddenly starting to rise. I caught sight of myself in the window and saw the look of ecstasy on my face and hoped that no one else was watching besides the brunette. My hard nipples were pressing against the loose cotton of my sundress, and if anybody had bothered to look up from their cell phones, it would have been obvious exactly what was going on below their line of sight.

I could feel my orgasm rising and I clenched my face to mask the intense sensations gripping my body. I couldn't believe I was about to come again surrounded by hundreds of oblivious passengers. Well, not *every* passenger. I saw the college girl's lips part and her eyelashes begin to flutter as she neared the peak of her own pleasure. Suddenly, her chest jerked in a series of small rhythmic spasms. Seeing her come as she watched the brunette fuck me from behind opened my own floodgates. A powerful orgasm engulfed my body as I clenched my ass cheeks together, clamping down over the brunette's hand between my legs. She watched my suffering in the window as my pussy squeezed her thumb in a series of violent contractions. My climax seemed to go forever and I twisted my face, trying to mask the incredible feeling of ecstasy washing over me.

The decibel level in the cabin suddenly escalated again as the train entered the next station, finally giving me a chance to exhale and catch my breath. I wondered if the college girl noticed the puddle of fluid on the floor directly underneath me and between her legs. By the time the train stopped, my pussy finally finished pulsing, and the brunette began to retrieve her hand from between my thighs. As passengers began exiting the train, I reached into my purse and handed her a handkerchief. She wiped her hand with the cloth, then placed it in her pants pocket and squeezed in front of me. I was disappointed she was wearing another pantsuit today, but I understood her intention clearly. There was no way I was going to leave her hanging for a second day in a row. I was dying to return the favor and give her a silent orgasm of her own.

But it wouldn't be quite as easy to disguise my attention, especially to the passengers seated directly in front of us on the bench. The college girl was flanked by two middle-aged businessmen reading the New York Times. If either one of them lowered their paper and looked up, they could easily detect the movement of my hand between the brunette's parted legs. The brunette must have been thinking the same thing, because she ducked under my outstretched arm and shifted over to my other side, directly in front of the college girl.

So she *had* noticed the girl's attention after all!

She reached up to grasp the overhead bar with her left hand and placed it next to mine. We'd switched positions now and I was the one who had clear access to her ass and nether regions with my dominant hand. When the train picked up speed and rocketed out of the station, I didn't waste any time. I didn't know what her regular stop was, but I looked up at the map and saw that the Javits Center stop was only four stops away. If I was going to get the brunette off in time not to miss the start of my conference for a second day, I had to get to work quickly.

When the train entered the tunnel, I moved my hand behind her ass and slipped my fingers into the crack between her legs. I gasped when I felt the moist opening of her bare slit. *Clever girl!* She'd opened the seam between her pant legs just enough for me to slip two fingers inside her. I glanced at her in the window and rejoiced as I thrust my middle and forefinger deep into her pussy. She closed her eyes and parted her legs as I felt her left pinky finger twitch on the bar next to mine.

From my new position two feet further to the side, I could now see the side of the college girl's face clearly. She was staring straight ahead, watching the movement of my hand between the brunette's parted legs. From her position directly in front of the brunette, she had a clear view of my fingers buried inside her pussy. She glanced out the corner of her eyes to ensure her seatmates were still distracted by their papers, then spread her legs gently apart. Her right hand then disappeared under her book, and when I glanced at the brunette in the window, I saw that her attention was also riveted on the girl.

I could feel the brunette's pussy growing wetter, and a soft moan emanated from her closed mouth. I smiled at the thought of her and the college girl sharing a moment, then I pulled my forefingers out of her pussy and inserted my pinky and ring fingers in their place. As I began to fuck her with my two little fingers, I pushed my forefingers forward until I found her hard nub pressing against her trousers. The college girl now had a commanding view of my fingers working the brunette's clit, while the rest of my hand fucked her hard from behind. I could feel the brunette's hips swaying as I pushed my fingers in and out of her, and the pace of her breathing increasing between her parted her lips.

Just when I thought I might be able to get her off before we hit the next stop, the train roared into the 72nd Street station. The businessmen on opposite sides of the college girl glanced up from their papers to check the station and I quickly retracted my fingers from the front of the brunette's pussy to ensure they wouldn't notice. As the passengers began to thin out beside us, I removed the rest of my hand, worried that someone might wonder what it was doing positioned so far under the brunette's ass.

It wasn't quite as easy to disguise our activity as it had been under my dress. I checked the subway map to see how long the distance was to our next stop at Columbus Circle. Then I looked at the brunette in the window and nodded, indicating that we'd have a little more time alone in the next tunnel. When I peered down at the college girl, I caught her glancing at me. I smiled at her, but she quickly lowered her head in embarrassment.

When the train left the 72nd Street Station, I glanced at

the two businessmen to make sure the coast was clear, then I inserted my fingers back inside the brunette's slit. There was something about this combination of finger action that was getting me turned on, and I hoped the brunette was enjoying it as much as I was. As I thrust my little fingers into her pussy, my two forefingers pinched her clit under her trousers and I began to thrust them forward and backward.

The brunette's mouth parted and her eyes flitted with pleasure. Her cunt clamped over my fingers as she fucked my hand with her swaying hips. I glanced at the college girl and saw that her lips were parted as she panted softly, watching me finger the brunette just inches away from her face. I knew the brunette would want to make this last as long as possible, but as the train neared Columbus Circle, the pace of her hip movements sped up and the walls of her pussy pressed tighter around my fingers. As we swung into the station, her eyes flew open and she locked eyes on me as a flush rolled over her cheeks and she jerked her hips in a series of rhythmic spasms.

I glanced at the girl and saw her mouth wide open in a silent gag, almost like she was about to be sick. But I knew it was a different kind of sickness she was feeling as she experienced her own private *petite mort*. Realizing I'd just made two beautiful women come together on a crowded subway train, my own pussy began pulsing in an involuntary orgasm. As our carriage rolled to a stop in the station, the brunette reached into her pocket and handed me my soiled kerchief. I held it to my nose briefly pretending to wipe my nose, then quietly cleaned my hands as I soaked up the sweet bouquet of our forbidden love.

Read More

ABOUT THE AUTHOR

If you would like to receive notification of new book(s) in Jade's Erotic Adventures, follow me at http://bookbub.com/authors/victoria-rush.

If you have a moment, please post a brief review on my Amazon book page at viewbook.at/nc . Even just a couple of sentences will help other readers find and enjoy this book as much as you hopefully did.

Follow, share, like, and comment at:

www.facebook.com/authorvictoriarush
www.pinterest.com/authorvictoriarush
www.twitter.com/authorvictoriarush
authorvictoriarush@outlook.com

Hope to see you again soon!